Rhiannon Ally

MOMMY, PLEASE Don't Go to WORK!

Illustrated by Wendy Leach

ASCEND BOOKS

www.ascendbooks.com

Requests for permission should be addressed to: Ascend Books, LLC, Attn: Rights and Permissions Department, 7221 West 79th Street, Suite 206, Overland Park, KS 66204

10 9 8 7 6 5 4 3 2 1

ISBN: print book 978-1-7323447-0-9

Library of Congress Control Number: 2018944759

Publisher: Bob Snodgrass
Editor: Teresa Bruns Sosinski
Publication Coordinator: Molly Gore
Sales and Marketing: Lenny Cohen
Design: Komondor Creative Agency

Author Acknowledgements: Special thanks to Peter Goldberg, Wendy Leach, 41 Action News/Scripps, my extended family and friends, and to the many women who've shown me how to balance work and family through the years.

The goal of Ascend Books is to publish quality works. With that goal in mind, we are proud to offer this book to our readers. Please notify the publisher of any erroneous credits or omissions, and corrections will be made to subsequent editions/future printings. Please note, however, that the story, experiences, and the words are those of the author alone.

Printed in Canada

To Roman, Camila, my husband Mike and our baby girl on-the-way.

To my wonderful mother, Carolyn, and to all working moms. You inspire me.
Stop letting "mommy guilt" make you feel bad.
You are doing a fantastic job juggling it all!
- R.A.

Hi, my name is Leo, and this is my little sister, Luci. Being a big brother is a huge job!

I like teaching her new things and how to stay out of trouble.

Like not
pulling our dog
McCoy's ears.
"Be gentle, Luci."

And I like teaching Luci the
colors of Mommy's flowers.
"This one is red. That's my favorite!"
"Pretty!" Luci said.

My favorite thing to do is play with the whole family: Mommy, Daddy, Luci, McCoy and me.

We love having picnics and playing at the park.
Although, sometimes things
don't go as planned.

Luci loves to swing,
and I love to climb!

"Have a good day. I love you!"
Mommy said when she dropped
us off at school.

"May we go to the park after school?" I asked.
Mommy said, "My loves, I'm sad I have to work
late tonight, but I'll be home before dinner.
Daddy will pick you up from school."

The next morning, I had an idea.
Luci and I would try to get
mommy to stay home! It was
time to be on our best behavior!
We ate all our breakfast.
McCoy helped.

After breakfast, Luci and I cleaned the playroom and put away all the toys.

Mommy said, "I'm so proud of you both!"

"Does that mean we can all stay home?" I asked.
"Mommy, PLEASE don't go to work," Luci cried.
"I wish I could stay, but I have a big project to finish at work."

Since yesterday's plan didn't work, we tried something else the next morning to see if Mommy would stay home. During breakfast, we threw food and then made a big mess in the playroom! Mommy was not happy at all.

"Leo and Luci," Mommy said, "I love you no matter how you behave. But, sometimes moms must go to work. It doesn't mean that we don't miss you.

"Now, let's get to school. You will clean this up tonight. You can't be late! There's work to be done for the big bake sale."

At school, we colored
signs for the bake sale.
Mine had a rainbow
over a slide!
The teachers told us that the
money raised from the
bake sale would help our
school buy a new playground.

After school, we had to clean up the playroom instead of playing.

Mommy didn't stay upset at Luci and me for long. She read our favorite books and Daddy sang a song after our bath.

Mommy came inside our school the next day
to see all the hard work for the bake sale.
In the kitchen, there was a huge mess.
The cookies were burned, and the cakes looked horrible!

"The ovens overheated! What should we do?"
incipal Berger asked Mommy. "If we cancel the bake sale,
we won't have enough money for a playground."
Mommy had an idea.

Mommy is a TV news reporter and can spread the news about the ruined bake sale.

She called the TV station and asked, "Please send a camera crew over to the school. They need our help!"

When the TV crew arrived,
Mommy interviewed me
for the news story.

"Leo, why is the bake sale
so important?"

"Mommy, this bake sale will raise money for our new playground. I'm excited for a fun place to play at school!" I said. "Thank you, Leo. The school has been working hard to raise money for a playground, but their bake sale is ruined. They need everyone's help. The bake sale is tomorrow!" Mommy said.

And help arrived!
A firefighter came with her
fire truck. "I saw the news story
on TV. I came to make sure the smoky
ovens were turned off! What else can I
do to help?" she asked.

A doctor came with a first aid kit.
She had her baby with her.
"Is anyone hurt?" the doctor asked.

One by one, mommies from all over town came to help with the bake sale. There was a police officer, a mail carrier, a nurse, a lawyer, waitress, plumber and many more.

Then the best surprise!
Our favorite baker brought a truck filled
with cookies and cakes and pies to
donate to our bake sale!

The bake sale was a HUGE success thanks to all the moms!

People saw Mommy's story on TV and came to buy cakes, cookies and other treats.

Principal Berger said, "Leo and Luci, you and your mom saved the day! Without her and the other moms, there wouldn't have been a bake sale. Now, we've raised enough money for our playground!"

Later at home, Mommy said, "There are lots of reasons mommies go to work. So many of us do the jobs that people need. My job is to share stories like what happened at the bake sale. Look at all the moms who saw it on TV and left their jobs to help."

"My favorite job is being your mom and it will ALWAYS be the most important. All moms love their kids more than work. I'll be there when you need me. I miss you when I'm away from you and will always come home."
Then she gave Luci and me a big hug.

The next morning Luci cried,
"Mommy, please don't
go to work!"
I held Luci's hand and told her,
"Mommy loves and misses us
when she is away, but she has
her job to do. She'll be home
after work."

For dinner that night we
made our own pizzas.
Luci's looked like a heart!
Daddy left his pizza in the
oven just a little too long!

"We saw so many important jobs that moms do.
Maybe I'll be a pizza chef
when I grow up," I said.
"Or a news reporter like you, Mommy!"
"One day, you both will have important jobs.
Right now," Mommy said, "just be Leo and Luci!"